A Stranger in Casey's World

by Kate Stormer

Illustrated by Tom Lowes

Goblin Fern Press
Madison, Wisconsin

A Stranger in Casey's World

A portion of the proceeds from this book will go to the Wisconsin Canine Search and Recovery Association, which is a nonprofit group of volunteer dog handlers formed in 1998.

For information or to order additional copies please contact

Goblin Fern Press, Inc.

3809 Mineral Point Road, Madison, WI 53705

Toll-free: 888-670-BOOK (2665) **www.goblinfernpress.com**

ISBN: 0-9647663-1-0

Printed in the United States
First Goblin Fern Press Edition: June 2004

10 9 8 7 6 5 4 3 2 1

Casey's World™

Welcome to Casey's World!
Casey would love to hear from you.

Please write to
Casey
c/o Goblin Fern Press
or e-mail her directly at
casey@caseysworld.net

You can also visit her at
www.caseysworld.net
to find out about new adventures.

On a very quiet street
in a very quiet town
lived a very noisy little dog.

Her name was Casey.
She was small and gray and soft to touch.

Casey and her sister, Reba, loved to play in their backyard.
They knew it was safe to play here because
there was a fence that went all the way around the yard.

"I am the luckiest dog in the world,"
Reba barked happily as she ran from the big oak tree to the fence and back again.

But Casey didn't hear Reba.
She was watching a man walking on the street in front of her house.

It was Casey's job to protect her house and her family
from any strangers,
and Casey did not know this man.

“Hey,” yapped Casey. “Don’t come into our yard! I don’t know you. You are a stranger.”
And the man just kept walking right past Casey’s house.

“There, that’s better,” Casey said. “Our yard is still safe.”
And Casey turned to walk back to the house.

BAM! Reba and Casey were both tumbling across the soft grass.

"I'm sorry Casey," cried Reba.
"I was running fast and I could not stop in time to miss you."
Casey stood up and shook all the grass and twigs from her gray fur.

"Watch where you are going," Casey yelped at Reba.
"You have to keep your eyes open all the time and watch out for others."

"OK," said Reba quietly. "I'll try."

After a while, Reba stopped playing with her ball and sat down next to Casey to rest.

“I’m glad winter is over and spring is finally here,” said Casey.
“It’s the perfect time of year.”

“I like spring, too,” added Reba. “There are new leaves on the trees, pretty flowers growing, cute little baby rabbits and squirrels everywhere, and lots of people walking and jogging past our house.”

“I don’t like walkers and joggers,” growled Casey.
“They are strangers, and we should never let strangers in our yard.”

“But they all seem so nice and friendly,” Reba said.
“They don’t seem mean or scary.”

“You can’t tell if a stranger is good or bad by how they look or act,” scolded Casey.
Reba gave Casey a quick kiss on her black wet nose.

“You’re really smart, Casey,” Reba said.
“I’m so happy that you are my sister.”

After a few minutes of rest, Reba was ready to play again.

"Hey, Casey. Let's go to the park and see our friends," Reba suggested.

"Good idea," answered Casey.
"Maybe some of the children will throw a ball for us to catch."

The park was filled with people and dogs, just as Casey and Reba had hoped.

"Hi Martin," Casey and Reba barked loudly to the fat yellow dog
who was lying in the shade of the tall slide.
His young owner, Bobby, was playing tag with the other children.
"Have you seen Garcia or Angel today?" Casey asked.

Garcia was a strong brown and white dog with soft sad eyes and not much hair.
When Garcia played, he looked like he was slapping away bugs with his big front paws.

Garcia never hurt anyone with his boxing paws.
He and his family came to town from a country called Mexico.

Angel was a small pretty white dog
with long hair on her tail and a face that everyone loved.

Angel was shy, and she didn't speak to the other dogs very often.
Her best friend was Jamie, the little girl who always came to the park with Angel.

Martin raised his head, yawned and said,
"Here comes Garcia now, and Angel is over by the swings."

"It's about time you two got here," said Garcia in his gruff voice.
"We've been waiting for you so we can play ball with the children. Let's go."

“Hi, Garcia,” yipped Reba. “We’d love to play ball. Come on, Casey.”
And Reba and Garcia began to walk away.

“Wait, Reba,” shouted Casey. “Look!”

And all three dogs looked over to the swings near the edge of the park.
They saw Angel sitting alone, her leash tied around a small tree nearby.

"I wonder where Jamie is," said Reba. "She's always with Angel."

"Something's wrong," said Casey.
"Angel would never be at the park without Jamie.
Let's go see what happened."

And Casey, Reba, and Garcia raced over to talk to Angel.

"Angel, where's Jamie?" asked Casey. And Angel started to cry.

"Oh Casey," she sobbed. "I don't know what to do.
A man we didn't know asked Jamie to help him find a lost puppy. He said that the puppy would be afraid of me, so they left me here. And now they are gone, and I'm so afraid."

Casey knew this was not good. This man was a stranger.
They had to find Jamie right away.

“Reba,” barked Casey quickly. “Run to Zack’s house and tell him what happened. He’ll know what to do.” And Reba raced across the park to get Zack, the oldest and smartest dog in the neighborhood.

Casey snuggled closer to Angel so she wouldn’t feel so alone.

“Don’t worry, Angel. We’ll find her,” Casey said. “Zack will know what to do.”

Jamie was six years old and had long black hair and deep brown eyes that were shaped like little flower petals.

Casey knew that when Jamie was a baby, she lived very far away in another country. She was called Soon Soon. Last year, she came from way across the ocean to live here with her new mom and dad. And they named her Jamie.

“Which way did the man and Jamie go?” asked Garcia.

Angel pointed to the small path that led into the woods.
Casey knew it was important to find Jamie quickly, so she ran toward the path too.

“Garcia, call out when Reba and Zack come back,” Casey shouted over her shoulder.
“Then we will all go find Jamie.” And Casey disappeared into the woods.

Soon Garcia and Angel barked wildly to Casey, “Reba is coming with a policeman!”

“That’s right,” thought Casey as she scampered back to Angel and Garcia. “Zack’s dad is a policeman, and he will help us find Jamie.”

And they all dashed down the path to the trees.

Soon they saw Jamie and the man. There was no puppy with them.

"Stop!" barked all four dogs at once. And Zack's dad sped past them to grab Jamie before she walked any further with the man.

The man was so surprised that he jumped into a small truck and drove away quickly.

Zack's dad pulled Jamie into his arms.
She held on tight and began to cry.

Casey, Reba, and Garcia all cheered when Zack's dad
carried Jamie back through the park and down the street to her house.
Angel followed closely at his feet, her tail now wagging happily.

“Thanks for helping save Jamie,” Casey said to Garcia.
And both Casey and Reba waved good-bye to him and left the park.

They ran to Zack’s house to tell him what happened and that Jamie was safe.

“That was quick thinking, Casey,” Zack told them, after Reba finished telling him the story. “It’s important to get help fast when you think a child is lost or in danger.”

“How did you know what to do, Zack?” asked Reba.

“When I was young, it was my job to help the police find lost children,” Zack explained. “And now my dad and I sometimes go to schools to talk to the children about staying safe and helping others who might be in trouble.”

“Wow,” whispered Reba. “That’s neat,” added Casey.

And Zack told them a few more stories about helping the police find lost children.

"Zack's a real hero," said Casey to Reba as they walked back to their house.

"I think you are a hero too, Casey," said Reba.

"You knew just what to do to find Jamie.
You sent me to get help and then you tried to find where the man took her.
And you made Angel feel better and less afraid."

“Gee, thanks, Reba,” Casey said. “Just remember that you should never go anywhere with a stranger, and never let anyone you don’t know into our home or yard.”

“What about squirrels?” Reba asked Casey, “Are they strangers too?”

And they both watched a big squirrel climb to the top branch of the tree in their backyard.

“No,” said Casey. “They aren’t strangers.
And I’m so proud of you for spotting the squirrel in our yard.
You are learning to keep your eyes open for something that is not quite right.”

“Wow! It’s fun seeing what’s different in our yard,” Reba said.

And Casey and Reba both ran into their backyard to play until it was time for dinner.

To stay safe from strangers, Zack says. . .

Bring a Buddy: Always have a friend or adult with you when you play, walk to school, or go anywhere away from your house. Do not walk through alleys, dark streets, or anywhere you would be alone.

Use the Phone: Learn your home phone number and call it if you ever get lost or need help. Also, it's OK to call 9-1-1 if you need help, or if your mom or dad needs help.

Make Noise: If someone you don't know wants you to go somewhere, don't go! Yell, make a lot of noise, and run fast to a friend's house, or to a place that you know is safe.

Have a Secret Code Word: Select a secret code word that only you and your mom, dad, or a responsible adult know. Then if someone tells you your mom or dad said it was OK to go with him or her, ask for the code word. If they don't know it, make a lot of noise and run away fast to a safe place. Choose a word that is easy to remember.

Pick a Meeting Place: When you go with your mom or dad or another grown-up to a place where there are a lot of people (like a shopping mall or theme park), pick a public place to meet just in case you get lost. Then if you get separated from your mom or dad, you should go to the special place and wait there until they come for you. Don't worry. . . they will be there very soon.

Follow Zack's tips to stay safe and well, and we will see you in Casey's next adventure.

Ponder Points™

"My Ponder Points™ are intended to inspire discussion and questions, boost creativity, and spark imaginations. I hope they will help each child better understand and enjoy my adventures, whether they read them or listen to them."

Have you ever seen a stranger? What does a stranger look like?

Tell me about a place that you know really well.
Has there ever been anything different about that place? What was different?

What does it mean to trust someone? Name someone you trust.
Does this person make you feel safe? What does that feel like?

What is a country? Do you know where Mexico is?
What is it like to have friends who are from a place that's different than where you live?

What would you do if someone asked you to help him or her find a lost puppy?

What would you do if someone whom you didn't know
told you that your mom or dad said it was OK for you to go with him or her?

What can you do if someone you don't know wants you to go somewhere?
What are some ways you can get far away from the stranger?
Can you show me how loud you can shout?

Tell me what a policeman looks like. Have you ever seen or talked to a policeman?

What can you do if you see your friend talking to a stranger?
Can you tell me how to get help if someone is in trouble? Can you dial 9-1-1 on the telephone?

Welcome to Casey's World Adventures!

Here are the first two books in a series of delightful doggy adventures by Kate Stormer. Illustrator Tom Lowes uses soft watercolor illustrations to bring the dogs and their two-legged friends to life, and into your heart. All Casey's books include Ponder Points™ to encourage discussion and spark the imagination. Great for children ages 4 to 9.

ISBN: 0-9722099-7-2

Casey's Unexpected Friend

Meet Casey, the bold and brassy little dog who will take you and your child on many exciting adventures. In this first Casey's World story, Casey finds that her perfect world is about to be turned upside down . . . by a happy, energetic, and totally adorable puppy.

ISBN: 0-9722099-9-9

Casey's Four Holiday Celebrations

In this learning adventure, Casey and Reba learn about four special holiday celebrations—Christmas, Hanukkah, Ramadan, and Kwanzaa. You will meet Zack, the smartest and oldest dog in the neighborhood. A must-read for every holiday home!

Casey's World™

Also Available

Casey's World books for older kids!

Follow Casey, Reba, and all their friends as they go on new adventures and find wonderful places to explore.

The books provide approximately 60 pages of reading fun, with illustrations throughout the chapters.

Watch Casey's World website for further announcements www.caseysworld.net

Get Casey's World books from local or online bookstores, at **www.caseysworld.net**, or directly from the publisher at **www.goblinfernpress.com** or 888-670-2665.

www.caseysworld.net